DANIEL O' STUDIOS

&

THE BASEMENT MONSTER

Presents...

Copyright

I AM THE

MIDNIGHT ROBBER

Written and Illustrated by Daniel J. O'Brien

TWEET TWEET TWEET

TWEEEEEEEEEEEEET!

TWEET TWEET TWEET

TWEEEEEEEEEEEEEET!

I am deh Midnight Robber!
Deh twilight's master and lord!

Dis lil' reveler demands respect,
and won't be ignored!

I'm rough and tough like leather,
and dresses ain't never been my ting!

If bullies want to poke fun at dat,
den brace for deh verbal arrows I go sling!

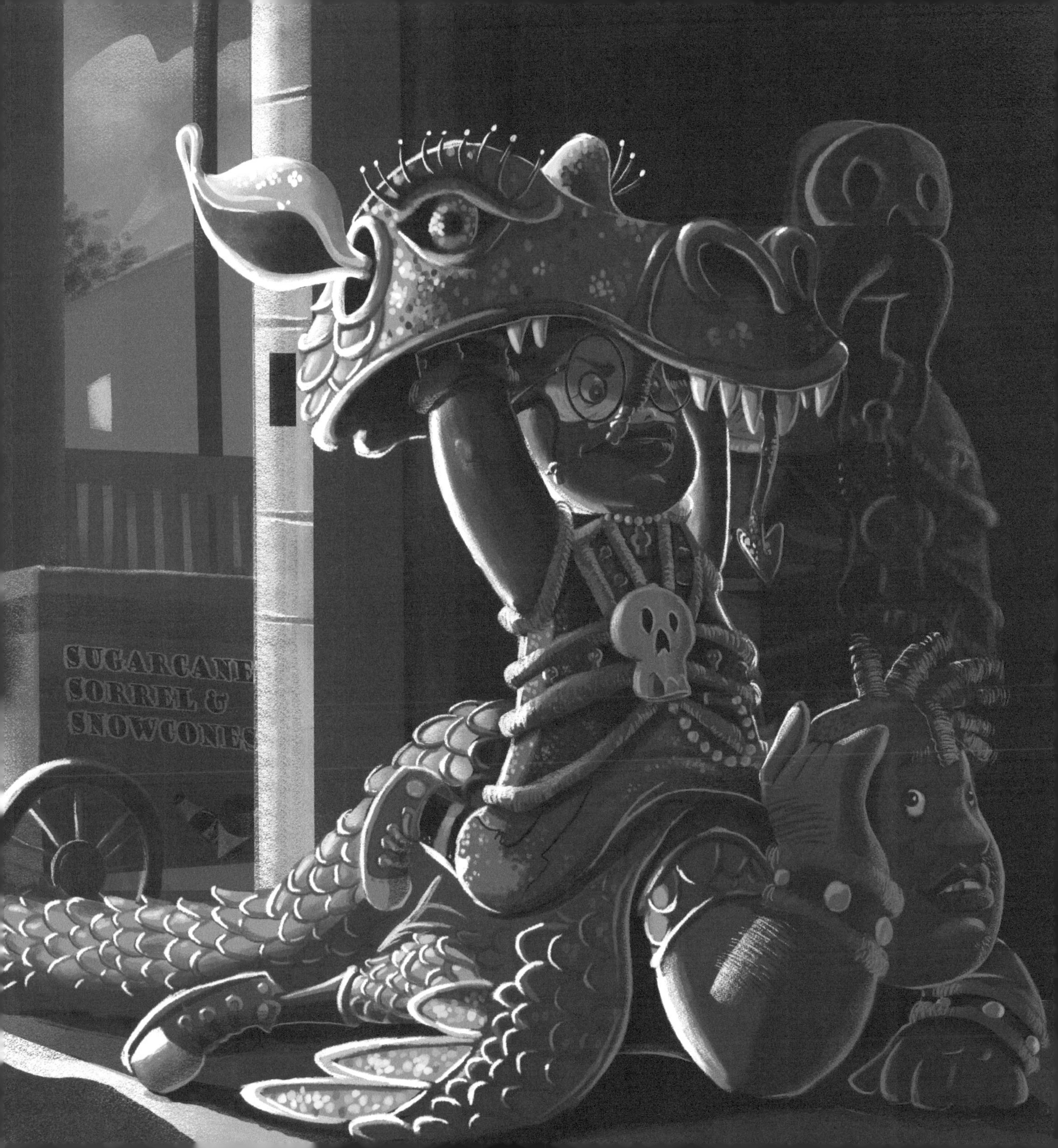
SUGARCANE
SORREL &
SNOWCONES

What yuh saying? Yuh never heard of
me and all meh wicked acts?

Well dis griots' gon' tell yuh a story,
and it starts with...

KRICK

CRACK!

Long ago dere was another Robber, whose
reign of terror was runner-up to mine!

Boy was so boldface, he swiped a ladder,
just to climb up and steal deh sun's shine!

Same time, dere was deh beautiful Dame Lorraine
who in a twist, stole deh Robber's heart.

From dat day forward, deh two masqueraders
vowed dat dey would never ever part.

 On deh next Carnival Monday, wedding bells rang and deh devoted couple became bride and groom.

A year later, Ms. Dame Lorraine was heard saying, "We may have to bid farewell to dis road real soon."

Deh happy couple gave birth
to me, deh cutest baby girl.

And in dat instant, yours truly
became deh masqueraders world.

But dat didn't stop deh revelers
from enjoying each carnival season.

Yuh bet we never miss a jump up,
and played mas in each and every region.

Dey named me after deh sweet sugarcane,
but I bit like a barracuda!

I was rough and tough like leather,
but yuh couldn't find a doudou any cuter.

When Daddy was not looking,
I would steal deh Robber's mask.

I would blow meh little whistle,
and take all meh enemies to task!

Mommy would try to fit me in dresses with
cute frills, pretty bows, and little top hats.

But MS. Dame Lorraine soon realized dat I,
lil' miss Sugarcane would be having none of dat!

Instead I reached for whistles,
toy skulls, and black hats on most days.

Mom and Dad couldn't help but think,
dis must be some sort of phase.

But of course it wasn't, and dey realized
dey didn't fully get me, their little girl.

But even though dey sometimes struggled,
dey never stopped trying to see my world.

With love and time dey understood dat me
dressing in Robber's guise was "No big ting."

And with dat thought in mind, dey looked forward
to what all future carnival seasons may bring.

But bullies became constant,
dey prodded and dey pricked.

Dere were many days where I felt
so mashed up and kicked.

But meh parents had meh back
through every bother and brawl.

Both, with a hand on meh shoulder
guided meh through it all.

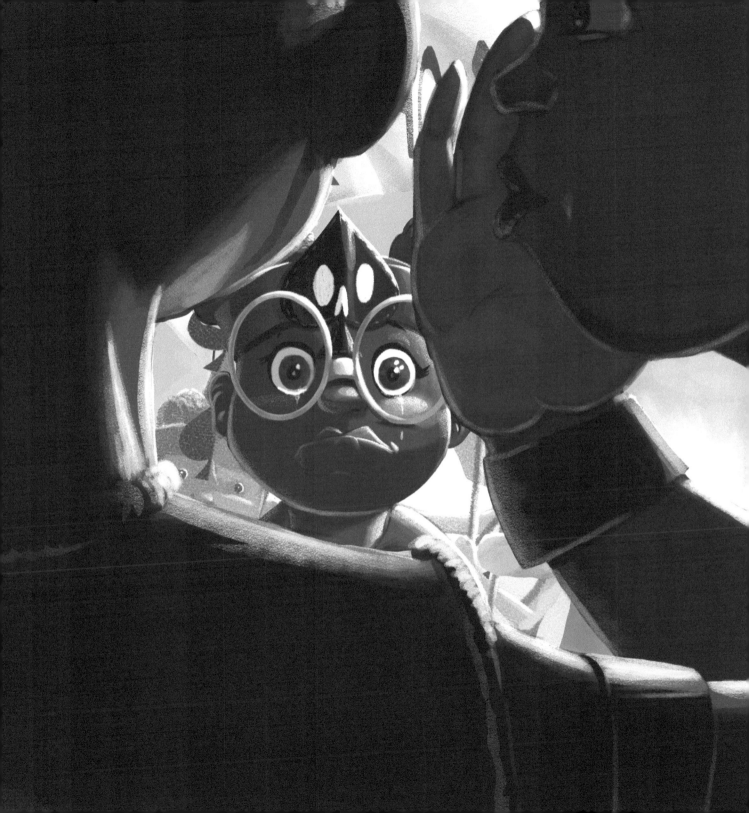

Dey told their lil' miss Sugarcane
not to "Bodda with all of dose people!"

Dey empowered me to just be myself,
and know dat I had no equal.

Dey would say, "Our girl is sweet like
sugarcane, but rough and tough like leather!"

"And in no way is it your fault
dat all dem macos refuse to get ya."

Dey helped me create costumes
and perfect deh Robber's rhyme.

I learned to steal deh hearts of millions,
one verse and line at a time.

Meh legend grew each month and year as I
masqueraded through deh streets.

I promised myself I would not stop
until deh whole world knew meh feats!

10th Annual
Robber Rumble!!!

I climbed to deh top of deh hill,
crushing all contenders along deh way!

And yuh bes believe it's on top of dis hill
I stand to dis very day!

WANTED

4 BEING
D BADESS!

Meh vest, meh hair, meh cape and soul
is black like Pitch Lake!

And meh rhymes are so yummy,
yuh tink dey be shark and bake!

Haha, yuh know I'm kidding,
I know it's bake and shark!

I've been schooled in meh culture,
and I ain't get no low marks!

With meh support by meh side,
I'll keep taking allyah to class!

While y'all play in sandboxes,
bes believe I'm playing in mas!

I will blow my whistle one more time,
asking, "Do allyah really hear me?"

For I am the Midnight Robber! public
enemy number one, two, and three.

TWEET TWEET TWEET
TWEEEEEEEEEEEEt!
TWEET TWEET TWEET
TWEEEEEEEEEEEEt!

The End

Until next time...

Midnight Robber

The Midnight Robber is one of the most well-known and well-liked traditional carnival characters. The Robber is known by it's costume, that includes a wide-brimmed hat and cape, and it's use of "Robber Talk": a boastful way of speaking, while speaking about all its bad deeds, adventures, and history. It is said that "Robber Talk" comes from the tradition of the West African Griot (storyteller). Robber Masqueraders often have a variety of skulls, weapons and coffins on them. Most importantly, they carry a whistles to grab your attention when blowing it! In the past it was usually men who played mas as the Midnight Robber character, but times are changing...

Dame Lorraine

People that masquerade as this character usually dress as large woman who wears a long dress and dances in the mas. This character was originally meant to mock the mas played by the 18th and early 19th century French planters, who would dress up in elegant costumes of the French upper class. They would parade in groups at their own homes, usually on Carnival Sunday night. They also performed the dances of the time. The freed slaves recreated these costumes in their own fashion, using materials that were readily available. Like the Midnight Robber, it was mainly men dressed as the Dame Lorraine character in the past. Lately, more women masquerade as the character.

GLOSSARY

Allyah (ul·ya): All of you people

Bake and Shark (bake·n·shark): It's a traditional fast food dish from Trinidad and Tobago. It consists of a deep-fried shark in between a deep-fried dough, called bake. The best-known place to purchase it is at Maracas Beach.

Bes (bes): Best

Bodda (bod·ah): Bother

Boldface (bol·face): To be Pushy, loud and wrong, unreasonable, demanding.

Chippin (chip·in): To march, shuffle, dance, and combo step alongside mas goers with similar costumes.

Dat (dat): That

Deh (dā): The

Dem (dem): Them

Dere (dir): There

Dey (day): They

Doudou (ˈdoō·doō): Sweetheart often used with darling, as in dodo dahling.

Jump Up (jump·up): The act of playing and dancing in Mas.

GLOSSARY

Krick Crack (krick·krack): A Caribbean oral tradition, call and response, meaning the beginning or end of a story or folktale.

Macco (mäkō): Someone who minds other people's business for the purpose of gossip

Mas (mas): When people dress in a wide variety of costumes for Trinidadian Carnival

Pitch Lake (pich lāk): Trinidad's Pitch Lake, located beside the village of La Brea, is the world's largest natural deposit of asphalt in the world.

Ting (ting): Thing

Tink (tingk): Think

Yuh (yuh): You

THANK YOU SO MUCH FOR READING!
If you enjoyed this book and are interested in seeing more
from me, DANIEL J. O'BRIEN, please head over to...

www.Daniel0Studios.com

@Daniel0Studios

@_Daniel0Studios

Daniel O' Studios

CPSIA information can be obtained
at www.ICGtesting.com
Printed in the USA
LVHW072016010221
678042LV00001B/1